D0116975

MOON ROOSTER

by David and Phillis Gershator
illustrated by Megan Halsey

MARSHALL CAVENDISH • NEW YORK

Text copyright © 2001 by David and Phillis Gershator
Illustrations copyright © 2001 by Megan Halsey
All rights reserved
Marshall Cavendish, 99 White Plains Road, Tarrytown, NY 10591

Library of Congress Cataloging-in-Publication Data
Gershator, David.
Moon rooster / David and Phillis Gershator
p.   cm.   Summary: When the youngest rooster on the hill decides it is his duty to bring up
the moon by crowing loudly each night, the people living nearby dream of rooster soup.
ISBN 0-7614-5092-0   [1. Roosters—Fiction. 2. Moon—Fiction.] I. Gershator, Phillis. II. Title.
PZ7.G314Mo 2001   [E]—dc21   00-064513

The text of this book is set in 15 point Frutiger.
The illustrations are collages.
Printed in Hong Kong
First edition

To poet Marty Campbell,
roosterman
— D. G. & P. G.

For Bruce
and his music
— M. H.

Dreamer

The youngest rooster on the hill couldn't sleep.

Insomniac

He stayed awake at night, thinking. **It's too dark**, he thought.
All the roosters bring up the sun, but not one brings up the moon.
Poor moon. If I can bring up the moon, it will light up the night!

The rooster knew what he had to do. "Cockadoodledoo," he crowed.

a peaceful sky

cockadoodledoo   cockadoodledoo

The moon did not rise.
Mister Rooster didn't give up. He slept all day long and crowed
at night, cockadoodledoo, and lo and behold, with one more
cockadoodledoo—

So the next night and every night after that the rooster crowed again, louder, cockadoodledoo, and the moon rose again, even bigger and brighter than before.

"Cockadoodledoo," he told the hens. "See what I can doodle do! I can bring up the moon!"

With one eye open, the big red hen watched the moon rise. "My, my," she said. "What you can do!"

Proud!

Moon Rooster's chest puffed out and his crown stuck up so bold and red, he was truly king of the hill.

The brown and white and spotted hens gathered around. "Cluck, cluck," they clucked. "What a voice! What a moon! It looks like a freshly laid egg!"

May

Kay

Faye

Bossy Red Hen

Moon Rooster crowed early,

cockadoodledoo

crowed late,

cockadoodledooooo

crowed all night long,

cockadoodledoooooo

He had a job to do,
and he did it,
proudly and loudly.

cockadoodledooOO

The people on the hillside appreciated Moon Rooster's hard work.
When he crowed with all his heart,
they *showed* their appreciation.
They threw gifts his way!

"keep quiet!"

The other roosters were amazed.
No one ever threw gifts to *them*.
Shoes, all sizes, big and small.
Pots and pans, flat and
deep. Clocks, tick-tocking
and click-clicking.
Rubber balls, and
even a bat
or two.

"We can't sleep!"

"Shush!"

For some reason, no one threw food. Moon Rooster would have liked a handful of corn kernels. No self-respecting rooster pecked at a rubber ball. Birds didn't eat leather or metal either, and the clocks were silly. The tick-tocking clock crowed long after the sun came up, and the click-clicking clock didn't crow at all. It chirped. A chirping clock couldn't rouse a cricket, let alone the sun and moon.

Ed

"No one ever threw me a gift."

Bossy Red Hen

Fred

Being a well-bred fowl, Moon Rooster crowed cockadoodledoo, thanking the folks for their gifts, silly or not.

Grateful

Ned

May

Kay

Faye

Then, one night, lo and behold and
cockadoodledoo, the moon
lit up the whole hillside.
A *full* moon, big and round!

A full moon,

"Come take my hand."

big and round !

It made the sea turn silver.
It made cactus flowers bloom.
It made the band play non-stop.
It made people sing and
dance til dawn.

Mary dances.

When the sun roosters crowed, and the sun chased the full moon away, one of the party people said, "Now that it's morning no sense in going to bed. But we'll get a good night's sleep tonight—*if* we can get rid of that pesty rooster!"

The others agreed. "Yes, let's catch that rooster right now, and cook him with onions!"

"Yes, and let's make chicken soup! Polly, run home and put the kettle on!"

A crowd of people charged up the hill waving pots and pans over their heads, shouting "Chicken soup!"

No one threw gifts to Moon Rooster. Instead, the people *chased* him. Why? They wanted to make chicken soup!

Moon Rooster didn't care for that dish, so he made getaway plans.

Moon Rooster flew up into the nearest tree and hid.

He hid until the people went home, to eat, to work, to do what people do. He hid until the sun slid out of the sky and sank deep down into the sea. High up in the tree, he whispered to himself, "Cockadoodledoo. Goodnight, sun. Cockadoodledoo. Goodnight, people."

Moon Rooster was worried and scared. For a whole week, he did not know what to do. Nearly losing his life had frightened him so much, he nearly lost his voice. He couldn't crow. He croaked.

Meanwhile, the moon got smaller and smaller—and then, it disappeared.

The night was dark and quiet, but Moon Rooster couldn't sleep. He stayed awake, thinking. *Poor moon*, he thought. *It can't come up. If I don't crow, who will make the moon rise and shine?*

The other roosters called to him. "Hello up there, Moon Rooster.
Why aren't you doing what you used to doodle do?"
And he croaked, "I can't."
"Why not?"
"I need help," he admitted.

where is the moon?

moon rooster is brave

Ed

Fred

At that, the other roosters stiffened their tails and puffed out their chests, and though they were still tired from their day job, they helped Moon Rooster bring up the moon. Cockadoodledoo, cockadoodledoo, cockadoodledoo, cockadoodledoo, cockadoodledoo, cockadoodledoo, cockadoodledoooooo.

Up from behind the mountains rose the moon, a thin, thin sliver of light.

With the other roosters at his side, Moon Rooster grew more courageous, and his voice grew stronger. The next night, he crowed once, twice, three times, and he didn't stop. Oh, no. He had a job to do. He had to bring up the moon.

Ned

a crescent moon!

What about those dark and quiet nights each month?
Well, Moon Rooster and his friends do such a good job,
sometimes they deserve a rest—and so does the moon.

And what about those sleepy people on the hill?

A few are still hungry for chicken soup, but most use earplugs. Besides, they know that if they catch one noisy rooster, another noisy rooster will take his place.

Why? Because *someone* has to bring up the moon, and if not for a noisy rooster, who will cockadoodle do it?

New Moon · Waxing Crescent · First Quarter · Waxing Gibbous · Full Moon · Waning Gibbous · Last Quarter · Waning Crescent · New Moon

Words and Music by David Gershator
Adapted by Yonah Daniella

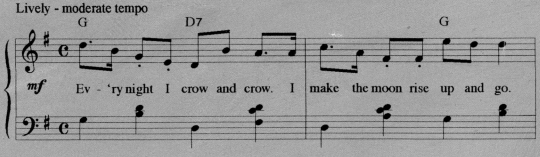

Ev - 'ry night I crow and crow. I make the moon rise up and go.

Cock-a-doo-dle doo, cock-a doo-dle doo. Up comes the moon for me and you. I

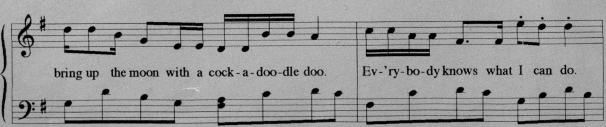

bring up the moon with a cock-a-doo-dle doo. Ev-'ry-bo-dy knows what I can do.

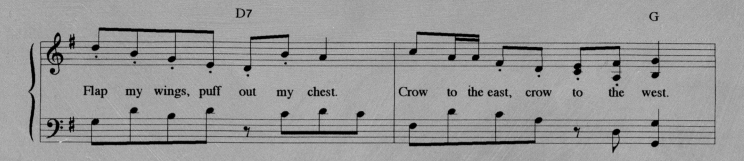

D7

Flap my wings, puff out my chest.

G

Crow to the east, crow to the west.

D7

Up comes the moon, shin - ing bright. Let's help the moon stay up all night.

G

D7

Flap your wings and cock - a - doo - dle doo.

G

You can crow the way I do.

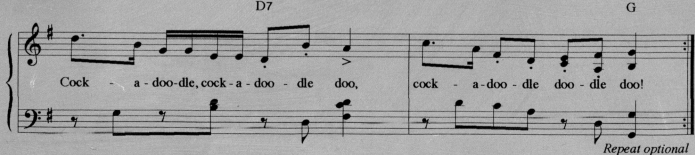

D7

Cock - a - doo - dle, cock - a - doo - dle doo,

G

cock - a - doo - dle doo - dle doo!

Repeat optional

dreams come true

THE END